STEPHANIE'S PONYTAIL
Story by Robert Munsch   Art by Michael Martchenko
CLASSIC MUNSCH

THE FIRE STATION
Story by Robert Munsch
Art by Michael Martchenko
CLASSIC MUNSCH

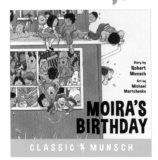

MOIRA'S BIRTHDAY
Story by Robert Munsch
Art by Michael Martchenko
CLASSIC MUNSCH

THE DARK
Story by Robert Munsch   Art by Michael Martchenko
CLASSIC MUNSCH

PURPLE, GREEN AND YELLOW
Story by Robert Munsch   Art by Hélène Desputeaux
CLASSIC MUNSCH

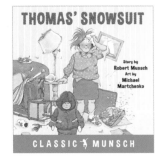

THOMAS' SNOWSUIT
Story by Robert Munsch
Art by Michael Martchenko
CLASSIC MUNSCH

I HAVE TO GO!
Story by Robert Munsch   Art by Michael Martchenko
CLASSIC MUNSCH

SOMETHING GOOD
Story by Robert Munsch   Art by Michael Martchenko
CLASSIC MUNSCH

MORTIMER
Story by Robert Munsch
Art by Michael Martchenko
CLASSIC MUNSCH

JONATHAN CLEANED UP — THEN HE HEARD A SOUND
Story by Robert Munsch   Art by Michael Martchenko
CLASSIC MUNSCH

ANGELA'S AIRPLANE
Story by Robert Munsch
Art by Michael Martchenko
CLASSIC MUNSCH

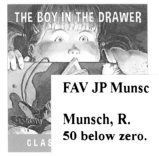

THE BOY IN THE DRAWER
CLAS

Story by Robert Munsch
Art by Michael Martchenko
MURMEL, MURMEL, MURMEL
CLASSIC MUNSCH

50 Below Zero

STORY by
ROBERT MUNSCH

ART by
MICHAEL
MARTCHENKO

annick press
toronto • berkeley

We acknowledge the support of the Canada Council for the Arts and the Ontario Arts Council, and the participation of the Government of Canada/la participation du gouvernement du Canada for our publishing activities.

Cataloging in Publication

Munsch, Robert N., 1945-, author
    50 below zero / Robert Munsch ; illustrated by Michael
Martchenko.

(Classic Munsch)
Previously published: 1986.
ISBN 978-1-77321-101-5 (hardcover).--ISBN 978-1-77321-100-8 (softcover)

    I. Martchenko, Michael, illustrator II. Title. III. Title: Fifty
below zero.

PS8576.U575F44 2019   jC813'.54   C2018-903650-8

Published in the U.S.A. by Annick Press (U.S.) Ltd.
Distributed in Canada by University of Toronto Press.
Distributed in the U.S.A. by Publishers Group West.

Printed in China

www.annickpress.com
www.robertmunsch.com

Also available in e-book format. Please visit www.annickpress.com/ebooks.html for more details.

To Jason, Watson Lake
and Tyya, Whitehorse,
Yukon Territory

In the middle of the night, Jason was asleep:
ZZZZZ—ZZZZZ—ZZZZZ—ZZZZZ—ZZZZZ.

He woke up! He heard a sound. He said, "What's that? What's that? What's that!"

Jason opened the door to the kitchen . . .

and there was his father, who walked in his sleep. He was sleeping on top of the refrigerator.

Jason yelled, "PAPA, WAKE UP!"

His father jumped up, ran around the kitchen three times, and went back to bed.

Jason said, "This house is going crraaazy!" And he went back to bed.

Jason went to sleep:
ZZZZZ – ZZZZZ – ZZZZZ – ZZZZZ – ZZZZZ.

He woke up! He heard a sound. He said, "What's that? What's that? What's that!"

He opened the door to the kitchen. No one was there.

He opened the door to the bathroom . . .

and there was his father, sleeping in the bathtub.

Jason yelled, "PAPA, WAKE UP!"

His father jumped up, ran around the bathroom three times, and went back to bed.

Jason said, "This house is going crraaazy!" But he was too tired to do anything about it, so he went back to bed.

Jason went to sleep:
ZZZZZ—ZZZZZ—ZZZZZ—ZZZZZ—ZZZZZ.

He woke up! He heard a sound. He said, "What's that? What's that? What's that!"

He opened the door to the kitchen. No one was there. He opened the door to the bathroom. No one was there. He opened the door to the garage . . .

and there was his father, sleeping on top of the car.

Jason yelled, "PAPA, WAKE UP!"

His father jumped up, ran around the car three times, and went back to bed.

Jason said, "This house is going crraaazy!" But he was too tired to do anything about it, so he went back to bed.

Jason went to sleep:
ZZZZZ—ZZZZZ—ZZZZZ—ZZZZZ—ZZZZZ.

He woke up! He heard a sound. He said, "What's that? What's that? What's that!"

He opened the door to the kitchen. No one was there. He opened the door to the bathroom. No one was there. He opened the door to the garage. No one was there. He opened the door to the living room. No one was there.

But the front door was open, and his father's footprints went out into the snow—and it was 50 below zero that night.

"Yikes," said Jason, "my father is outside in just his pajamas. He will freeze like an ice cube."

So Jason put on three warm snowsuits, three warm parkas, six warm mittens, six warm socks, and one pair of very warm boot sort of things called mukluks. Then he went out the front door and followed his father's footprints.

Jason walked and walked and walked and walked. Finally he found his father. His father was leaning against a tree.

Jason yelled, "PAPA, WAKE UP!"

His father did not move.

Jason yelled in the loudest possible voice,
"PAPA, WAKE UP!"

His father still did not move.

Jason tried to pick up his father, but he was too heavy.

Jason ran home and got his sled. He pushed his father onto the sled and pulled him home. When they got to the back porch, Jason grabbed his father's big toe and pulled him up the stairs:
BUMP, BUMP, BUMP, BUMP.

He pulled him across the kitchen floor:
SCRITCH, SCRITCH, SCRITCH, SCRITCH.

Then Jason put his father in the tub and turned on the warm water.
GLUG.
GLUG,
GLUG,
GLUG,
GLUG,
The tub filled up: GLUG,

Jason's father jumped up and ran around the bathroom three times and went back to bed.

Jason said, "This house is going crazy. I am going to do something." So he got a long rope and tied one end to his father's bed and one end to his father's big toe.

Jason went to sleep:
ZZZZZ – ZZZZZ – ZZZZZ – ZZZZZ – ZZZZZ.

He woke up! He heard a sound. He said, "What's that? What's that? What's that!"

He opened the kitchen door . . .

and there was his father, stuck in the middle of the floor.

"Good," said Jason, "that is the end of the sleepwalking. Now I can get to sleep."

In the middle of the night, Jason's mother was asleep:
ZZZZZ – ZZZZZ – ZZZZZ – ZZZZZ – ZZZZZ.

She woke up! She heard a sound. She said, "What's that? What's that? What's that!"

She opened the door to the kitchen and . . .

Even More Classic Munsch:

The Dark
Mud Puddle
The Paper Bag Princess
The Boy in the Drawer
Jonathan Cleaned Up—Then He Heard a Sound
Murmel, Murmel, Murmel
Millicent and the Wind
Mortimer
Pigs
The Fire Station
Angela's Airplane
David's Father
Thomas' Snowsuit
I Have to Go!
Moira's Birthday
A Promise is a Promise
Something Good
Show and Tell
Purple, Green and Yellow
Wait and See
Where is Gah-Ning?
From Far Away
Stephanie's Ponytail
Munschworks: The First Munsch Collection
Munschworks 2: The Second Munsch Treasury
Munschworks 3: The Third Munsch Treasury
Munschworks 4: The Fourth Munsch Treasury
The Munschworks Grand Treasury
Munsch Mini-Treasury One
Munsch Mini-Treasury Two
Munsch Mini-Treasury Three
Classic Munsch ABC
Classic Munsch 123

For information on these titles please visit www.annickpress.com
Many Munsch titles are available in French and/or Spanish, as well as in
board book and e-book editions. Please contact your favorite supplier.

More MUNSCH to enjoy!

SHOW AND TELL
Story by Robert Munsch
Art by Michael Martchenko
CLASSIC MUNSCH

PIGS
Story by Robert Munsch Art by Michael Martchenko
CLASSIC MUNSCH

DAVID'S FATHER
Story by Robert Munsch Art by Michael Martchenko
CLASSIC MUNSCH

WAIT AND SEE
Story by Robert Munsch
Art by Michael Martchenko
CLASSIC MUNSCH

The Paper Bag Princess
Story by Robert Munsch Art by Michael Martchenko
CLASSIC MUNSCH

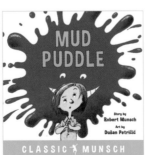

MUD PUDDLE
Story by Robert Munsch
Art by Dušan Petričić
CLASSIC MUNSCH

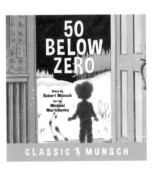

50 BELOW ZERO
Story by Robert Munsch
Art by Michael Martchenko
CLASSIC MUNSCH